Unboxed

Unboxed

Non Pratt

Barrington Stoke

First published in 2016 in Great Britain by
Barrington Stoke Ltd
18 Walker Street, Edinburgh, EH3 7LP

www.barringtonstoke.co.uk

Text © 2016 Leonie Parish, writing as Non Pratt

The moral right of Leonie Parish to be identified as the
author of this work has been asserted in accordance with the
Copyright, Designs and Patents Act, 1988

A CIP catalogue record for this book is available
from the British Library upon request

ISBN: 978-1-78112-585-4

Printed in China by Leo

For my friends who contributed to the "Time Capshoole" — the ones I see every few months and the ones I haven't seen for years, there isn't a day I don't think about you.

1

Ben

It seems worse to break a promise to the dead than it does to break one made to the living. Why else would I be standing by the gates of my old school waiting for a bunch of strangers I used to call friends?

Ben, Dean, Millie, Zara. Me – Alix. Five friends, five years … it feels like a lifetime.

My phone lights up with a message from Faith.

Anybody there yet? x

Only me. Is it too late to flake out?

Need me there for moral support?

Her offer makes me smile. Everything that girl does makes me smile.

Tempting ... but I don't want to be one of those girls who can't do anything without their gf.

No worries. I'm on the Diet Coke tonight, so give me a call if you need me to pick you up.

I love you. **xxx**

I know. (insert imaginary Han Solo emoji ...) xxx

I'm still smiling at my phone when there's a weird growling noise near by. When I look up, I nearly wet myself.

"What the fuck!" There's someone standing in front of me and I press one hand to my chest as if to stop my heart from hammering. My other hand locks my phone and slips it safely into my pocket.

"Sorry. It's me, Ben – Ben Buckley," he says. As if there might be some other Ben coming tonight. "Sorry if I scared you. That was why I coughed."

"That was what it was? You sounded like a goddamn bear."

He looks like one too. The Ben I remember was
always a little broad, but the one I'm looking at
now is big. Tall and chunky, his belly filling out his
T-shirt as much as his chest.

"Huh," he says. He's staring at me the same
way I'm staring at him. "You've changed."

"A bit. So've you." I'm not sure why I'm being so
defensive. I don't *think* he was trying to insult me.

"I meant from your profile picture. Your hair."
Ben nods at my head. "Suits you."

My hand goes up to my hair. I'm always
changing it. Cut, colour ... the only thing I'm
consistent with is that it's never longer than my
jawline. Not since I was thirteen, in fact.

Ben is exactly the same as he is in the many
pictures he's posted online. Of all of us, he's the
easiest to find, username 'BenjiBucky' on every
social media site in existence. His Insta is packed

with pictures of him and his friends, the animals he walks past, the food he's eating, the places he's going, the clothes he's wearing. Ben isn't seeing anyone – if he was, there'd definitely be pictures of them kissing.

Ben and I never had much in common.

"So, are the others coming?" Ben asks. "I mean, apart from ..." He waves his hand in some kind of sign-language for 'Millie'.

"Zara is." Who can say what Dean will do? He doesn't seem to exist online and he never replied to the email I sent.

"Zara ..." Ben says with a reverent shake of his head. "Man, I've not seen her in ages. How is she?"

But I've not seen her either. I suppose Ben thinks we're all in touch one way or another, still here after he moved with his mum to London. He comes back to see his dad in the holidays – I've seen him out sometimes, hanging with the lads he used to play football with. Loud shirt, loud laugh, Ben makes himself hard to miss, but his people are not mine and I've never stopped to say "Hi".

I'm aware that I'm giving off unfriendly vibes, shutting down every avenue of conversation before it starts, and so I ask about London, hoping to get Ben talking so I don't have to. It works. He starts going on about how busy it is, how you can get the bus or the tube or the train anywhere you want any time of night or day, how cool the clubs are, the bars and the shops. He talks about London like it's half a world away and not 42 minutes on the fast train.

There's the sound of an engine at the end of the road.

"Does Zara drive?" Ben asks.

Like I'd know.

"Whoever's in that car, I doubt it's Dean," I say.

2

Zara

The car pulls over. It's one of those high-end 4x4s, so big that Zara seems tiny by comparison as she steps down from the passenger seat. But I was wrong to assume it was her dad who'd given her a lift. The man getting out of the driver's side is *definitely* not Mr Joshi.

I resist the urge to roll my eyes when Zara nestles into him as they walk together towards the school.

When Zara sees us, she squeals in joy and peels away from her other half to run over and fling her arms around me.

Surprised, I hug her back, taking in how small

she feels. She's all hard edges and pointy joints.
If I squeezed too hard, she'd snap. She doesn't
go to hug Ben. Instead, she darts a glance at her
boyfriend before she grabs Ben's hands. She has
her elbows locked to keep him at arm's length.

"Benji! Oh my God, I can't believe it's you!"

It's like watching a dried pea size up a
marshmallow.

"Hi, Zara." Ben's focus shifts to the boy behind
her and he lets go of Zara to hold out his hand. "I'm
Ben."

Zara's boyfriend leans in and clasps Ben's hand
like we're in a boardroom. "Ashish Dutta," he says.

Apparently his name should mean something,
because he's waiting for a reaction. Ben and I
exchange the same clueless look.

"Ash's dad owns Dutta Developments," Zara
explains, as she cosies up to her boyfriend once

more. "Ben's been living in London for the last few years," she tells him. "And this is Alix."

"Hi, Ash." I wave. No way am I shaking anyone's hand. "Are you dropping Zara off or ...?"

The smile remains fixed on Zara's face as she says, "You guys don't mind if Ash comes along, right?"

Ben and I make indistinct "Of course not" noises because it's not like there's an alternative.

Changing the subject, Zara asks Ash if the knot on her halter-neck has come loose. She then twists round, trying to see over her own shoulder.

"Yeah," Ash says, but he makes no move to help. Instead he turns to Ben, who asks him whether he's at university. He looks old enough.

"Here," I say to Zara, stepping closer to sort out the problem.

When Zara lifts up her hair I catch a waft of

lemons and basil and cedarwood. It's strange how a scent can be so instantly familiar. It twists time so it seems like yesterday that we were sitting in my room, Zara cross-legged in front of the mirror as I piled strands of her thick dark hair up, pinning them to the crown of her head, while Zara chattered about how excited she was to be allowed out. We were only going to the cinema.

Tonight she's dressed for somewhere more exciting than the cinema – silk top, skinny jeans. Statement jewellery. The only thing that's missing is a pair of heels that she probably left in Ash's car.

"All sorted," I say, and I double-knot the bow.

"Thanks." Zara smiles brightly at me and I feel a pang of something like guilt.

"You guys going somewhere nice after?" I ask.

"Bullion. You ever been there?"

I shake my head.

"If you buy a cocktail they rim your glass with edible gold glitter," she tells me.

"I don't really drink cocktails. Too pricey."

"That's why you get a guy to buy them for you!" Zara giggles, and the sound flutters out as pretty and delicate as a dragonfly as she looks at Ash.

The pang of guilt is much sharper this time. There was more than one reason I didn't want Faith to come along tonight.

I never had to worry about my family when I came out. Mum has always been aggressively liberal and my not-so-little brother Evan thinks anything that's different is cool. But I worried about my friends. When people mean something to you, it matters what they think. Hard as I find it now, these guys were everything to me back then. I worried that if I wasn't the person they thought I was, then maybe *they* weren't who I thought either? It made me ill. Ill enough that I got signed off school and never went back – not to Downham, anyway. We'd always lived between this town and the next, so it wasn't hard for me and Evan to switch schools and switch lives.

It's weird. I've been out for years. I've kissed girls in dark corners, held hands under tables. I've sat in the common room at college and laughed about embarrassing dates, sharing my stories without holding back, not worrying what anyone thinks. I've had my heart broken and I've had it healed.

But tonight, I have travelled back in time and into the closet.

I am thirteen again and worried what my friends will think.

3

Dean

I can't tell whether the thrill I get when I see Dean is because I'm pleased to see him, or because of all the things I've heard about him.

Dean Marshall was always a little dangerous. He was skinny and surly and had really cool hair. He could riffle shuffle a deck of cards, skim a stone up to five times across the surface of the sea and raise one of his eyebrows into a perfect arch.

He was everything I wanted to be and, even now, there's a part of me that asks what thirteen-year-old Dean would think when I do something cool.

Eighteen-year-old Dean stops a short distance

from where we're all standing with his hands in his pockets and his shoulders slumped forward. His hair's been buzzed around the sides and he's lean, but you wouldn't call him skinny in case he glassed you for it.

"All right," he says, with a nod.

Still just as surly.

Zara doesn't show him the same affection she showed us, and even Ben 'I live in London' Buckley seems reluctant to step forward with a handshake the way he did for Zara's boyfriend.

"Hey, Dean." I do my trademark half-wave in greeting. "Didn't know if you'd come."

"Neither did I." Dean studies our little group. "Haven't seen you guys in a while." His gaze rests on Ash. "Millie's changed."

It's a pretty dark joke that shocks a laugh out of me and a frown from the other two. Ash reacts by looming a little larger over Zara and saying, "I'm Ash. Zara's my girlfriend."

He doesn't bother with his surname the way he did for me and Ben, like he doesn't think it would mean anything to someone like Dean. I think he's wrong. Dean's family has always made it their business to know everyone else's.

"So what do we do now?" Ben looks at me for an answer. Again. It's not like he couldn't work it out for himself.

"We go get the box," I say with a shrug.

"Wait a minute," Ash says. He's staring at me, but talking to Zara. "I thought she was the one who sent the email?" He doesn't wait for Zara to confirm before he addresses me. "So you don't actually have this box you want everyone to open?"

"No," I say. "I don't."

"So why did you organise all this?"

"I didn't."

But that's all he'll get from me. I turn away to walk along the fence line. I'm tired of answering everyone's questions. Zara must have told Ash why we're here – if he needs more explanation, she can be the one to give it.

None of us expected things to change the way they did. Less than a week after we made the box, Ben's mum walked out on his dad and took Ben with her. It was my turn to leave next, then Dean's – out of Downham and into a pupil referral unit. Zara lasted until sixth form, when she got a scholarship for the posh all-girls college.

Only Millie stayed here for the full five years. Or she would have, if she hadn't died three months ago.

Millie was the only one I still talked to – she was always interested in other people's lives, even if those lives weren't very interesting. The emails and messages she sent when I moved schools went from a steady stream to a thin trickle, to a sporadic drip here and there, but they still came, even if I didn't always reply.

Until she sent one with the subject –

Cancer (mine)

I push the memory away.

"Unless you guys know the combination for the lock on the gate, this is the best place to get in," I say. I show Ben and Dean where the wire's come away from one of the fence posts.

Ben isn't happy. "Isn't there another way?"

"You'd prefer to climb over, would you?" Dean says. There's a smile in his voice, even if there's no trace of it on his face and Ben turns a little pink.

"What are you trying to say?"

"That this is the only way we can all get to the

other side," I reply before Dean can say anything less tactful. "No one can get over the fence without a leg-up, which means someone would have to stay on this side while we went in and someone else would get left behind on the way out."

It's like one of those maths problems where you have a dog, a cat and a mouse trying to cross a river in a boat that'll only take two at a time and none of them can be trusted not to eat the other.

The boys look blank before Dean says, "What Alix said."

We wave the other two over, but Ash insists on walking the length of the fence himself, before he admits that this is the best way in.

"And after you're inside, then what? There'll be cameras and alarms –"

Dean stops him. "No there won't." Ash isn't happy at being interrupted, but Dean has zero fucks to give. "Alarms and CCTV are only a problem if you try and go inside the building."

Ash frowns, baffled. "So where *are* you going?"

It's Ben who points up at the roof. "*On* it."

4

The roof

There was something deliciously illicit in climbing onto the roof after Summer Club, listening to the staff gossip once the little kids had been collected and they thought no one could hear. Up there, away from the edge, you're invisible to anyone on the ground and if any of the neighbours noticed us from their bedrooms, they never reported it. Dean's brother told him about it – we found an old pack of his cigarettes hidden in one of the air vents with the lighter tucked inside. We dared each other to smoke one. It did not end well.

We used to climb onto the bins by the kitchen and scale the wooden slats of the bike shed. From the bike shed it's an easy climb onto the flat roof of the main building.

Or at least it used to be.

"When did they replace the bike shed?" Ben asks.

Yet another question he thinks other people can answer.

The five of us stand in a line and survey the brick wall of the school's latest extension. The surface is painted smooth in a disgusting salmon pink and the bins are nowhere to be seen either, presumably relocated inside the pink-bricked monstrosity. We split up and walk round the school hunting for an alternative. Ben and Dean head one way, me, Zara and Ash the other. I'd rather be with the boys, but there was something in the way Zara's shoulders drooped that swayed me. But now I'm here, walking two paces behind them, I'm not sure why I bothered.

Ash is talking about how badly planned everything is. I switch off and watch the way Zara rolls her hips with every step, the channel of her spine running between the peaks of her shoulder blades. Everyone else has grown with age, but Zara seems smaller.

Ash turns to look at me. "Didn't you think to scout the place out first? How long is it since any of you were here?" I don't have an answer. Zara goes to say something, but Ash carries on. "At least Dean seemed to know what was what."

This nettles me enough to actually say something.

"About the cameras?" I say. "And the alarms?" Zara shoots a warning look at me that I ignore.

"Dean would know all about that," I say. "He's the reason the school installed them."

"What do you mean?" Ash asks, but he's already thinking along the right lines – he has been ever since he set eyes on Dean.

"Three years ago someone smashed all the windows in the sports hall and set fire to the library. It was after my time, but ..." I give Zara a look heavy with meaning ... "wasn't that around the time Dean was excluded?"

Zara frowns and turns to point at the school. "Do you think we could climb up this fence and onto the overhang by that classroom?"

We drop the subject of Dean in favour of studying the fence and I experiment with hooking my fingers and jamming my toes into the holes in the wire. It's not easy, but maybe with a leg-up, it could work.

I jump back down and nod. "Let's tell the others we've found a way up."

Before I can go anywhere, Ash holds out a hand with the palm forward, as if I'm an over-excited dog. "You girls wait here," he says. "I'll go get the lads. It'll be faster."

Faster than what? I want to ask him. *Can my flimsy female fingers not type Ben's number as fast as your manly meat stacks can carry you?*

But Ash is already jogging off round the school. There's an unnecessary bounce to his step that my sports-science girlfriend would say creates impact and adds stress to his joints.

"He's nicer when you get to know him," Zara says. "Ash can be a bit ..."

"... of a tit?" I suggest.

Zara laughs, more heartfelt than before. "I was going to say 'up himself', but you kind of summed it up." She sighs. "He's sweet when it's just me and him, but he can be a bit much around other people. Especially people he wants to impress."

"Ash wants to impress me?" I point to myself in case there's any doubt who I mean by the word 'me'.

"He wants to impress my friends."

I'm not sure whether that does mean me or not. "Well, he's very, er, tall," I say. "And handsome."

"Do I need to worry about the competition?" Zara asks.

"Not from me," I blurt out so fast it sounds rude, especially since Zara was joking. Then I add, "Really not my type."

It's the perfect time to tell her, to breeze in with something like, "You think Robin Hood is the fox, but it's Maid Marian does it for me." But I'm not breezy around her, or any of these guys. I'm buttoned right up, hiding who I am.

"Why did you say all that about Dean and the brick through the window?" Zara asks. "I thought you guys were close?"

I ignore the second question and answer the first. "Because it's true, isn't it? Everyone said he did it."

Zara stares at me and I can feel my shell harden under her gaze. All the little things I've been telling myself seal the cracks ... *she doesn't need to know, it's not like we're friends any more, you don't have to see any of them after tonight ...*

Ben's voice carries across the playground from fifty paces and we turn to watch their approach.

"How would you have known what everyone was saying?" Zara asks in a low voice. "You weren't even there."

5

The box

Only two of us make it up onto the roof – me and
Dean. Ash declared he never had any intention of
trying and Zara caught her silk halter-neck on the
wire and got very upset about how much it cost.
Ben was keen, but isn't built for climbing – although
without a leg-up from him to the top of the fence,
I'm not sure we'd have got here either. Dean and I
aren't as athletic as we used to be.

I step away from the edge towards the middle
of the roof, and the others are swallowed up and
hidden from view. Without their presence pressing
on me, with a summer sunset blazing out across the

sky above, I feel free, light as a feather, as if I could float off and leave them all behind.

But Dean's here, tying me down.

"What now?" he says.

"Why does everyone think I have a plan?" I say. I can't keep the irritation from my voice, even though it's the first time Dean's looked to me for an answer. Unlike Ben and Ash, and even Zara, who act like this is all my idea.

"We don't," Dean says. "We think Millie had a plan." He stares at me, harder to read than Zara – harder to read than any of us. "And we think she told you what it was."

But I made Millie a promise, not a plan.

"*Promise you'll try, Alix,*" she'd said. "*They'll come if you ask them.*"

"*They'll come if* you *ask them,*" I told her.

"*By the time the holiday starts, it'll be the same*

thing," Millie insisted. "*My question, your voice.*"

I'd not known what to do when she said that. Perhaps if we'd stayed in touch more I'd have felt comfortable giving her a hug, or holding her hand. Instead I just squeezed her foot, propped up next to me on the sofa. And I'd promised, not really believing it would ever come to this. Death was something that happened in other people's stories.

Not mine. Not Millie's.

My eyes feel as hot as my heart when I think of her mum pressing *send* on the email Millie had written to tell us it had happened.

"I don't think Millie had much of a plan for getting the box," I tell Dean, burying my grief deeper inside. "She thought the hard part would be getting us to meet up."

We both know she was right. Neither of us was a safe bet on that front.

I squint against the sun at Dean as he looks out over our old territory. What does this boy, this almost-man, remember of the time we spent up here making memories that couldn't be whittled down into words and stored in a box?

"Let's go," he says and he starts walking towards the dark grey square in the middle of the roof that marks the courtyard between the upper school and the lower. When we get there, we stare down at the paving slabs, the benches donated by old pupils and local service clubs. The box is hidden in one of the ventilation bricks around the edge, but neither of us remembers which one.

We go to the first corner.

"This doesn't feel right," I say.

"No." Dean frowns across the courtyard. "None of this does."

"You mean without Millie?"

"Yeah," is all he says, before he walks round to the next corner.

But I don't think that's all he means. Of all the people here tonight, Dean's the most like me, closed off and quiet. Maybe he's like me in other ways too. Maybe he's struggling to remember why we were all friends in the first place, wishing he hadn't come, wanting to be with the friends he has now – or someone closer?

"Weird how Zara brought her boyfriend along," I say.

Dean shrugs. "Not really." Which I assume puts an end to that, but then he says, "Zara likes belonging to people."

"You mean boys?" It sounds more snide than I meant it to.

"I mean people," he says. "Family. Boyfriend. Friends ... You."

This brings me up short. That isn't how it seemed to me, not at the time and not now. Zara was my closest friend at school, before we fell in with the others, but Zara had never *belonged* to me any more than she belonged to anyone else.

Dean's stopped walking. He nods across the courtyard to where a metal grille is winking gold in the last of the daylight.

"Over there."

It's only after we've worked out which ventilation brick it is that it occurs to me what we need to do to get inside. Dean looks at me and the arch of a single eyebrow triggers years-old envy.

"Your turn, Alix," he says, and hands me a penknife.

6

Extraction

My shoulders hurt where my vest's digging in as I hang upside down in it like a harness. Dean's holding onto the back of it with his weight braced to stop me from falling.

Was it really this dangerous when we did it before?

Thankfully there are only two screws holding the grille in place and they come out more easily than I was expecting. The grille clangs on the courtyard below.

"What was that?"

Dean must have leaned forward because my shoulders dip slightly.

"Just the grille!" I shout. "Stop leaning over!" Most of me remains on the roof, but I'm still very scared of falling. It was Dean who put the box here before and I'd have preferred it if he was the one getting it out again. Back then Ben was the one doing the bracing while me and Millie sat on Dean's legs and Zara faced the other way so she wouldn't see what happened when we fell.

If I tried to hold onto Dean, we'd both be splats on the paving slabs by now.

Bending my arm round is hard. My elbow isn't exactly designed to bend that way and I try not to think of the gritty, sticky, cottony things my fingers brush against as I reach inside the shaft behind the brick. When I touch the smooth surface of the box it catches me by surprise and I jerk back so that I graze my knuckles on the brick. I grab the handle and try to tease it out. Every bump and scrape shoots arrows of agony along my arm and into my shoulder.

When at last I get the stupid thing out, I hang there for a moment, enjoying how it feels to have my arm pointing in the right direction again.

Dean gives a sharp tug on my vest. "You coming up, or what?"

Back on the roof, we sit on one of the air vents and study the box. It's locked shut with a cheap combination padlock. Dean reaches over and starts rolling the numbers round.

"Two-two-eight," he says with a thin-lipped smile. "My birthday."

We needed a number we'd all remember and Millie had suggested the date we decided to make the box. The date we'd stood outside the door to

Dean's flat, daring each other to be the first to knock, until his dad flung the door wide open and we'd all screamed. Even Ben.

"We're calling for Dean." I'd been surprised to hear my voice doing the asking. *"We want to wish him happy birthday."*

All of us were scared of Dean's dad and when he turned away to call for his son, we released a collective breath out in the corridor. Later that night, high on sugar and the adrenaline of too many fairground rides, we sat on the sand banks and stared out to sea and Dean told us it was the best birthday he'd ever had.

"I wish I could fold it up and put in a box, y'know?" he'd said. *"Keep it safe for the rest of my life."*

When we put the box together, the card we'd made for his birthday was one of the first things to go inside.

Before Dean has a chance to open the box, my phone starts buzzing in my pocket, then blares out 'Happy' as I stare at the screen. It's Ben. Dean understands my eye-roll as I answer.

"Yeah, all right we're com–"

"Someone's here!" Ben hisses into the phone.

And even though there's no reason to, I duck down. "Who's here? The police?"

Dean stiffens beside me. "The police are here?"

I shush him because Ben's talking low and fast and I need to focus. I nod as I listen and then hang up.

"One of the neighbours must have seen us," I say. My heart is already thumping at the prospect of getting caught. "There's a van parked up the road and a couple of men in uniform came in the gate."

"What uniform?" Dean runs his thumb over the

lock on the box to jumble the numbers. He looks
worried.

"Ben's certain it's not the police," I say. Dean
doesn't seem reassured and I babble on. "Zara and
Ash had already gone back to the car to wait, but
Ben's hiding in the trees by the Lower School. He
reckons it'll be faster if we get down onto the roof
of the library and jump from there onto the ground.
Then we can bolt for it across the playing fields –
there's that cut through to the main road. The
other two will meet us there."

A cut that will be sealed off by a gate as secure
as the one across the main entrance. Dean grits
his teeth and shakes his head like he thinks it won't
work, but we both know there's little choice.

My phone goes again.

"They're walking round the other side of the
building – now's your chance!" Ben's voice is

charged with excitement – he's enjoying the drama.

I hang up. "Go, go, go!"

We dash across the flat roof, bending low, making ourselves harder to see from the ground. Dean's got the box and I've my phone out in case Ben calls with further intelligence. As I run towards the edge, a manic brand of joy builds in my chest.

Maybe I've got more in common with Ben than I thought.

"Down!" Dean hisses and he seems to melt into the roof in front of me as I stumble and sprawl forward. I dislodge a clump of moss with my chin, and gravel scrapes my skin, tumbling down my vest and into my bra. We commando crawl towards the edge, my vest scooping up more gravel, until we're close enough to peer over.

I'm grinning, but when Dean turns back to me, he's far from amused. I guess it's hard to find the fun in running when you know what happens if they catch you.

It's a short drop from here to the pitched roof of the library, where the tiles slope down towards the pre-school playground beyond. Dean nudges me and points to where there's a little playhouse just beyond the edge of the roof. His meaning is clear. The library is too high to jump straight down – better to leap from library to playhouse to ground.

My phone goes and I press it to my ear.

"Where are you?" Ben says. "You won't have long before they get round here ..."

Instead of wasting time arguing, I hang up and nudge Dean.

"Now!"

In a scrabble of gravel we try to get down. Dean's faster than me. He rolls onto his front, swings his legs over the edge and drops down onto the library roof. I'm still dangling over the edge when I feel hands on my hips steadying me and I let go. The tiles are steep and slippery and if it weren't for Dean, I'd have fallen and rolled off the roof like a pebble.

"Thanks!" I gasp.

But Dean's already pulling me with him. Our feet thunder on the roof as our legs race to keep up with gravity and I'm forced to let go of his hand to leap over the skylight. I kick a tile loose as I land, sending it tumbling ahead of us to smash on the ground below. My phone's singing in my hand, my toes straining against the ends of my shoes and I'm running out of roof …

I jump, a giant, ungainly leap, limbs flailing, legs stretched in a giant stride.

One weightless, noiseless moment and then I thump onto the roof of the playhouse. My feet, legs, chest squash together like a concertina and my free hand grasps at the ridge of the roof too late so that I tumble onto the ground.

"ALIX!"

Dean's sailing over my head and I've no time to get out of the way before he slams into the roof of the playhouse. With a creak and smash, the walls cave in, taking Dean with them.

7

Escape

Dean rises from the wooden ruins with blood blooming from a gash in his arm, but he's come off better than the little house. There are shouts from around the corner.

"We've got to go!" I yell.

"The box ..." Dean kicks splintered planks away as he looks down at his feet. "I dropped it."

The sensible part of my brain says to leave it, but that's not the part that's in control of me tonight. I hurry over to sift through the wreckage of the playhouse, even as my feet yearn to run.

"There!" I bend over and pull the box from

under a toddler-sized cooker that seems to have survived the impact. "Come on!"

I tug at Dean's T-shirt as the security guards appear round the side of the school. They break into a run when they see us.

"Shit!"

With that one word, Dean leaps out of the house and sprints at a pace I couldn't hope to match across the field towards the cut. A second later and I'm running after him, my phone still clamped in my hand, box swinging around in the other. My arms pump as fast as my legs, my heart, my blood. There's another figure running along the hedge-line to my left – *Ben*. I think how stupid he was to wait up by the school, until I remember him calling to tell us when to go for it, acting as our eyes on the ground as if we were some kind of black ops team from *Call of Duty*.

Stupid, but loyal. I feel a flash of affection that's at once familiar and forgotten.

Dean's at the cut, turning to find out where I am, yelling at me to run faster, and I make the mistake of twisting round to see two men a lot tighter on my heels than I expected.

"Stop there, young lady!"

I dig deep, sucking as much air as possible into my lungs, and put on an extra spurt of speed. I get to the path the same time as a pink and panting Ben, who stops to push me ahead of him into the narrow gap between the houses on either side of the path. Dean's ahead of me, crouched down by the gate, hands cupped ready to give me a leg-up. Without thinking, I push one foot into his hands and throw myself up as far as I can. I drop the box on the far side, and haul myself over the railings.

On the other side, Ben skids to a halt.

"How are you going to get out?" he says, chest heaving.

"I'll climb. Come on, mate!" Dean urges as I start shouting.

"They're coming!"

Ben tries to pull himself up. Dean shoves him from beneath, getting a foot in the face as Ben flips himself over the top. And then Dean's pulling himself up, fingers clamped round the railings, one leg braced against the wall to the side, the other scrabbling for purchase on the smooth metal of the gatepost.

The guards are half way down the path when an engine roars behind me and a pair of headlights flares full beam down the dusk-lit alley. The lights surprise the men chasing us just as Dean yanks himself up and over and out of reach.

"Get in!" Zara's yelling from the passenger

window and the three of us run round to the back of the car, scrambling in, slamming the doors behind us. Dean's on the floor, Ben and me on the seat and we all lurch back as the engine revs and Ash reverses in a swift curve that sends me sliding into the door. Ben's bulk is flung against me before Ash slams his foot down and we're speeding away from the school and the men who are no doubt going to report us for vandalising a kids' playhouse.

In front of me, Zara turns round. "Did you get it?" she asks.

8

Regrouping

When our fear of being followed has faded, Ash pulls into a supermarket car park and the three of us in the back squash together on the seat. I'm in the middle with Dean on my left, smearing blood over me, and Ben is perspiring gently on my right. There are bits of grit sticking to the skin between my breasts and I resist the urge to dive a hand into my cleavage to fish them out.

Instead, I pull a paper napkin from my back pocket. My bum squeaks on the leather seat and makes Ben snigger, but Dean is too busy frowning at my napkin to join in.

"Use it to mop up the blood," I say, and I shove it into his hand. "Or you'll stain the seats."

At this, Ash turns round sharply. "Fuck! No bleeding in my car!"

"Sure, I'll just stop then." Dean rolls his eyes, but he presses the napkin over his wound. I tell myself that there's no reason to think he just recognised the name of the gay pub in the next town over, printed on the top corner. Or that he'll jump to any conclusions if he did.

"You don't think they saw us, do you?" Ben looks out of the rear window.

"Er, yeah," I say, then I add, "Even in the dark it's hard to miss that shirt you're wearing."

My wit is rewarded by the worried frown he gives his jazzy, short-sleeved shirt.

Ash looks far from happy in the front. His jaw is set as he jabs at the controls for the air-con.

"I don't think they'll have had time to get the number plate," I say more seriously.

Ash ignores me, but Zara turns round with a small, grateful smile. "It's not like you were fleeing the scene of a crime," she says. "Not a proper one."

Dean and I exchange an uncomfortable look that none of the others seem to notice.

"So where now?" I say brightly, keen to change the subject. "When we open the box, we should have a little more ceremony than Morrisons car park."

Zara starts to suggest we go somewhere to eat, but her sentence fades away when she notices her boyfriend. For all her claims that Ash wants to impress her friends, it's clear he'd rather not be seen with us.

"How about we drive up to the church where they buried Millie?" I say.

At once the mood in the car shifts from excited

to sombre and I regret my suggestion.

Ben looks out of the window. "The church feels a bit grim," he says. "But Alix is right, we should include Millie. Pick somewhere we'll remember her."

There's a different sort of quiet in the car now as we reflect on the times we spent together. My mind casts outwards, from the school to the cinema, beyond the far edge of town to …

"The play park."

Dean says it just as I think it.

9

Journey

It's Ben who suggests we get supplies and, fifteen minutes later, the four of us return to where Ash is waiting. I'm pretty sure from his expression that he'd have driven off if his girlfriend wasn't with us. Zara gets out the plasters and vodka and tells Dean to stand still while she pours a little over his arm and wipes it off with what's left of the napkin.

"Don't waste too much on this loser." Ben punches Dean lightly on the other arm to show he's joking, and Dean smiles back. The dynamic between them has changed since Ben stayed back and Dean hoisted him over the fence. It's as if the years apart have been bridged by a tentative trust.

I feel it too.

When we climb back into the car, Ash dodges
the kiss Zara leans over to plant on his cheek.
There's something acutely sad about the way she
glances round to see whether anyone's noticed –
something even sadder in how fast I look away.

"Where to?" Ash says as he fires up the engine.
Zara says she'll direct him. Her voice is low as she
looks down at the box.

"Didn't we put some music in there?" Ben says,
craning over me to see. "Open it up!"

"I thought we were waiting?" I argue, but
Zara's already clicking the numbers into the right
combination – two-two-eight. She opens the box to
reveal a flash drive taped to the underside of the
lid.

"Just this!" She holds the flash drive aloft and

shuts the box again. "Anyone got something we can play it on?"

But Ash has reached over to pluck it from her grasp. He plugs it into a USB port by his knee and flicks the volume up with the switch on his steering wheel.

At once a deafening beat blares out and Ben and Dean whoop in unison, their fists pumping the air.

"TUNE!" Ben shouts. He elbows me in the boob as he moves his hands up and down in time to the beat.

There's no mistaking whose choice this was and I meet Zara's eye as she turns round again. I don't know about her, but I've not listened to this song since that summer – a one-hit remix that came back from Ibiza clubs only Ben could name. Wherever we were, he would find a way to crank the volume up when it came on, even asking if the girl behind the counter at a café could turn the radio up, just for one song. Because it was Ben – charming and enthusiastic and persuasive – no one ever said no.

Dean hasn't been this animated all night. Even at the school, when he was shouting my name and jumping off the roof, his face remained calm, his expression under control. But now, next to me, when the song ramps up for the bridge, his face is split open in a huge grin, eyes crinkled up in joy.

He looks so *young*.

"Whose song's next?" Ben resorts to his old habit of asking questions no one can answer, but then the drums start up and I yelp in delight.

"It's mine!"

And it's so stupid, because I've got this song on almost every playlist, but I'm in the first flush of lust for it once more, bopping about as much as my seat belt can take. Ash's posh car becomes our dance floor, as all four of us – me, Zara, Ben and Dean – break into co-ordinated drumming and clapping and air-bass-playing to the intro for 'Blue Monday'. After the first thirty seconds, their enthusiasm wanes. Zara says to no one in particular, "It goes on a bit, doesn't it?" but no one suggests skipping it and we listen on as Zara directs Ash away from the coast road and up into the hills.

"It used to take us ages to get out here," Ben says and I nod, remembering how we'd get off the bus at the bottom of the hill and walk up, the five of us spread out in a line taking up the whole road. Like so many things we did without thinking, it was ridiculously dangerous – it's a narrow, winding road with high hedges. Even Ash is driving like a Nana in a Nissan – and he overtook every car possible on the road out of town.

The park is half way up the hill, miles from the

village it serves and there's no cars in the layby next to it. Ash is about to kill the engine when Zara holds out a hand to stop him.

"Wait, I want to see what's next."

A couple of simple guitar chords start up and it takes me exactly as long as it does everyone else to work out whose song we're listening to.

10

Park life

"When I die I want them to play this at my funeral," Millie told us.

It didn't seem morbid at the time. Back then we were obsessed with our own deaths because our lives were taking so long it seemed we'd never reach the end of them.

We were in Millie's room, just the three girls, because Ben was flaky and Dean ... well, we never asked too much about what stopped him from spending all his time with us.

None of us liked to think about his dad, least of all Dean.

"*It's a bit cheery for a funeral, Mills,*" Zara said, but Millie hadn't cared.

"*Death's part of life, no need to get all down about it,*" she announced.

But it was a comment that came from the privilege of never having lost a loved one. None of us had, no matter how often Zara insisted that the funerals of her two rabbits and a hamster had broken her heart and soul.

"*I want to be cremated,*" I said. "*They can play the* Terminator *theme tune as my coffin rolls into the flames. Duh-duh DUM-DUM-DUM. Duh-duh DUM-DUM-DUM.*"

And the three of us had burst out laughing, rolling round on our backs on Millie's floor doing terrible Arnie impressions and trying to claw ourselves across the floor with one arm.

That day we wrote down our 'wills' and swapped

them around – Zara's to me, mine to Millie, Millie's
to Zara – so that even if we died, our wishes would
live on.

Now, all these years later, I meet Zara's eye and
she nods, just once.

When Dean's choice comes on, he's the first to
suggest turning it off. "I can't believe I ever liked
this crap," he mutters.

Whatever bond we built on the school roof has
been lost. Dean's face is shuttered again, eyes cold,
mouth tight. He turns to get out of the car, leaving
me to climb out the other side, where Ben's holding
out a hand to offer help I don't need.

"What song do you think Zara chose?"

Another Ben Buckley special that I don't know
how to answer as we follow the others. Weeds have
split the surface of the path and Ash touches a hand
to Zara's elbow to steady her. The jacket she's now

wearing looks like something Faith would like and I wonder where she got it from.

I think back to when we were thirteen, trying to sort the hits of that summer from all the others that came after. Whatever Zara chose, it would have been something popular. Zara's tastes shift with the times.

"I don't know," I say. But I've spoken too soon. "Wait ... something with female vocals." I'm surprised I remember.

"Guess we'll find out on the way back." Ben keeps in step with me, his hands jammed down into the pockets of his shorts, his feet bouncing a little with every step. He seems less pompous than he was earlier. It was often like this between us. I would get annoyed at him until he shucked off the personality he wore around his other friends and brought out the real Ben – the cheerful, curious, outward-looking Ben that I thought of as my friend.

The park used to look old, but sea-winds and salt have aged it to ancient now. Paint has flaked off some of the rides to expose the steel beneath, and time has bleached the red rubber swings to an insipid pink. There are weeds everywhere, and grass growing up around the edges of the rubbery surface that's lost its give. But the view hasn't changed a bit.

A sweeping vista of fields leads down to the town, buildings huddled round the mouth of the river, the sea a grey whale-skin stretching out to swallow the world. Everything's lit up – warm yellow windows in the houses, sodium lamps and shop signs, the disco-glitter of the arcades and the soft swoops of the red lanterns that light the promenade and the pier. A town putting on its jewels ready for the night ahead.

Zara nearly drops the box when a crow flaps out from the shadows inside the climbing frame. She laughs it off almost immediately.

"Oh-mi-god. Stupid bird!" she says, breathless, one hand on her heart as she grins at me and Ben.

In a single, long-forgotten reflex Ben and I reply, "You are." We look at each other, the same surprised smile on our faces.

"Hey!" Ash steps forwards and lays a hand on Ben's shoulder, voice as low as his brows. "What did you just call her?"

Ben takes a step away, and Ash tightens his grip. To his credit, Ben doesn't seem particularly intimidated. "All right, mate," he says. "It was just a joke."

A joke rooted in our group history, a line we spouted out every other sentence whether it was an insult or a compliment, or just plain stupid.

Dean – Your ringtone is really annoying. Ben – You are!

Zara – My tea's too hot. Millie – You are!

Millie – I don't like the sea. It's too wet. Me – You are!

A joke I made too – a fact Ash is ignoring so he can prove himself the alpha male.

"You are bang out of order – *mate*," he growls. "No one takes the piss out of my girlfriend."

"We weren't," I say. I lay a hand on Ash's arm, alarmed at how solid the muscle is beneath his skin.

"Ash!" Zara's protest has no effect and she rolls her eyes. "Ash! Stop it. No one was insulting anyone."

Ash holds Ben in a predator's glare, then shoves his shoulder as he lets go and turns to follow Dean.

"I wish he wasn't so over-protective," Zara says. She's watching Ash so she doesn't notice the look that passes between me and Ben. "But it's nice to know he cares."

"Not so nice for us," Ben mutters.

Zara's shoulders tense beneath the soft leather of her jacket, but she walks on as if she hasn't heard.

❚❚
Photo album

We sit in a ring around the wooden floor of the roundabout.

Zara's tucked between Ash's splayed legs, her back against his chest as she places the box in the middle of the circle. Dean unscrews the cap of the vodka and takes a swig before he passes it to Ben, who wipes the bottle with the corner of his shirt before sipping a little and screwing his face up.

"Didn't we buy some Coke to go with it?" he asks.

"We have to make space in the bottle," I say. "Which will take hours if you carry on like that."

I take the bottle and gulp some back, ignoring the scorch of alcohol up my nose.

"Zara?" I offer.

"No thanks." She waves it away, even though she was the one who paid for it.

"Are you ever going to open that box?" Ash says and we all look from one to the other.

Now the time has come, I realise how little I want to do this. Tonight has already dredged up feelings – what's inside the box will only push me further towards a truth I'm reluctant to face.

Everyone's staring at me when I look up from the lid of the box.

"You do it, Alix," Ben says. "You're the one Millie asked."

I wish she hadn't.

I open it up, and lift out the note that's resting on top.

PRIVATE

This box and its contents are the property

of Alix Smith, Ben Buckley, Dean Marshall,

Millie Freberg and Zara Joshi.

Of the email addresses listed below, only Ben and Millie's are still the same.

When I put the note down, everyone, even Ash, draws in a little closer to peer at what's underneath.

Mostly just envelopes.

"Man, do you remember how obsessed Millie got with the envelopes?" Ben says.

The flash drive that's still in Ash's car was taped to the top of the lid, but everything else has been secured in envelopes numbered one to five. We take them out and arrange them in a circle around the box until we get to the photo album at the bottom.

"Album first, then an envelope each?" I say without thinking. Five friends, five envelopes. That was our plan when we put everything in, never imagining what would happen before we took it all out.

"Yeah," Ben says quietly and I'm grateful to him for not pointing out the flaw in my plan. "Let's do that."

Zara's the one who reaches for the album and we all shuffle round to sit next to her. Ash gets up and mumbles something about making a call. Perhaps he's realised at last how odd it is for him to be here.

Sitting together like this, looking into the past, it's as if we've travelled back in time. When Zara opens the album, we're greeted with a mirror image of us looming over the lens against a blue-sky background. It's so convincing that I glance up, half expecting to see Millie's ghost sitting next to me.

"I've got a double chin!" Zara mutters. "That's the worst angle ever for a photo."

I sense more than see Ben's resentful glare. "At least you look better now than you did at thirteen."

"You look beautiful, Benji." I blow him a careless kiss across the circle. It's the sort of thing Millie would have done and I look at her laughing out from the photo, hair blowing across her face and catching in her mouth.

Dean remains silent as he turns the page to a whole spread devoted to me and I blush at being faced with so many pictures of myself.

The others think it's hilarious. They all point to one where the camera's caught me mid-scream after someone (my guess is Dean) has thrown a bucket of water over me. Zara marvels how long my hair used to be and Ben gets his revenge for my jab at his hideous shirt by mocking the knock-off T-shirt with the typo 'Spongeboob Squarepants' I'm wearing in all but one of the photos. Dean just smirks at the album and then at me.

"You were such a dork back then."

I pull a face. "Better than being one now." But all that does is intensify his smugness.

Ben's next, and I enjoy reminding everyone that he threw up six hotdogs seconds after we took the photo in which he's so pleased for having eaten them.

Dean's pictures aren't as easy to laugh at. He had an uncanny knack of striking a film-star pose whenever the camera was on him, squinting off into the middle distance and looking tough.

Zara looks up for permission before she turns over to Millie's page. I doubt any of us are ready, but there's a comfort in being together.

Millie looks perfect in all her pictures – a perfection that's far from beautiful or poised. In one of them she's pointing to an enormous red spot on her chin and underneath she's written *Schubert, my second head.* In another she's poking a blue-stained tongue at the camera and crossing her eyes. In fact, there's only one picture in which she isn't pulling a face. It was taken here, in the park, at the top of the climbing frame. She isn't looking at the camera, but out at the horizon, her profile sharp against the distant grey-blue of the sea.

"How can you miss someone you haven't seen for five years?" Ben says quietly. The way his eyes rest on that last picture makes me think that he must have been the one to take it.

"We all miss her." There's a catch in Zara's voice and I hand her another of the napkins stashed in my back pocket. I look up at Dean, whose attention has moved from the photo album to the napkin. When he feels me looking, he meets my eye with small smile and a quirked brow.

He knows.

But all he says is, "Next page."

Zara is as gorgeous as you'd expect in all her pictures, a younger, fresher beauty. Back then she considered mascara and lip gloss to be enough. It's all she'd need now – the careful contouring that looks so great in a selfie at a cocktail bar looks a little plastic in person.

If she were my girlfriend I would make a point of telling her how beautiful she was the moment she woke up, when she was reflected in my gaze alone, before the world could whisper its lies through the mirror.

A beauty like Zara's doesn't need polish to shine.

Does Ash ever tell you how beautiful you are?

But I can't ask her that.

The other pages are a mish-mash of weekends on the beach, here at the park, on the roof at school, at Summer Club ... There are several pages of candid photos taken when we went to Alton Towers. From the moment we got off the Club minibus, Ben dragged us round the most vomit-/terror-inducing rides – when they pulled us out of the queue for Nemesis to get the bus home I honestly thought he was going to cry.

So much of my life is digital – selfies saved on my phone, or holiday 'albums' copied into files on Mum's laptop – but I never take the time to go through them like this. Millie was the one who insisted on printing them out. I'd been the first to grumble about the waste of time and money, telling her we could see them whenever we wanted on her computer.

"What if something happens to my computer, Alix? What if some evil internet hacker infects my hard drive with a terrible virus that destroys the files as it eats away at the memory?"

I'm glad she ignored my complaints. A virus isn't the only thing that can eat away your memory.

The last page is another picture of the five of us. A dance at the Summer Club we'd hated when the holiday began, that had brought us so close by the end. We'd met at my house and Millie had asked Mum if she'd take a picture. I have the 'real' one tucked away in a box of old school stuff, the one where we're all smiling for the camera. This one must have been taken first, before we were ready. Dean and Ben are standing with their arms slung over each other's shoulders. Dean is reaching over to adjust Ben's (over-the-top) bow tie, and the pair of them are laughing as Millie turns to say something. Next to her, in a foreshadowing of tonight, I'm focused on the back of Zara's halter-neck as she lifts her hair up, tendrils as thick as jungle vines falling down to frame her face.

It's completely unposed and it's completely perfect.

12

Envelope no. 1

Ash has finished his call and returned to the roundabout. He isn't happy at how far along we are. (Or aren't.)

"I said we'd meet everyone at Bullion in an hour." He looks at his watch, then at Zara. "So if your friends want a lift home ..."

"We're right here, Ash, you can ask us yourself." My voice is sharp, but then I remember why it was we were in his car at all and add, "Thanks for the offer, but I'm fine walking."

Dean nods as he swigs more vodka and Ben murmurs, "Yeah, we're good."

Which leaves Zara.

"I don't think we'll be much longer," she says, tugging her jacket around her. "I'm sure no one will mind if we're a little late."

It's clear that Ash will, but instead of forcing the issue, he picks up the padded envelope with '1' written on it and hands it to Zara. "Crack on then."

Zara pulls open the flap, tips the contents onto the roundabout and reads out the note.

"'This envelope contains the one thing each person thought summed up the holiday.'" She smiles up at Dean. "It says this was your idea, so I think you should go first."

Dean laughs, a gentle chuckle, and picks up his item, a birthday card. On the front is a picture of a kitten that we'd drawn over with marker pens, adding clothes and accessories and a speech bubble with "I'm the birthday pussy!" that makes me cringe. Dean opens the card, and as he squints in the long-faded light at what's inside, his face softens and the tense jaw and tight line of his mouth relax into an easy half-smile.

It is the best of him I've seen all night, and I tilt my phone up and snap a photo before he can stop me. His joy is a wolf emerged from a mountain forest ... one second and then it'll be gone.

Dean hands the card round the others until at last I get to see what we'd written – an explosion of different colours, doodles and messages.

Millie's birthday wish emerges from the mouth of a cartoon goat for some reason, Ben had written a creatively lewd poem, Zara a lovely message listing all the things Dean did that made her laugh. And then there's mine – *I think you're brilliant.*

I look up to see Dean watching me read and I smile. It's a nice thing to say to someone and I'm pleased to have been the one to say it. Most people told him he was being disruptive, that he was lazy, stupid, vulgar, nothing but trouble. One day, I'd drawn the short straw of running up the stairs to the Marshalls' flat, and I'd heard Mr Marshall yelling behind the door. He was swearing at Dean – at his wife too – using language I didn't think existed outside of gangster films.

My fist had halted half an inch from the door, then I'd turned and run back down the stairs to tell the others that Dean couldn't come out.

I've regretted it ever since.

Ben's item is a collection of ticket stubs from every time we visited the cinema. There's at least three stubs from different showings of the same film and we laugh at him for going so many times because we couldn't all make one showing together.

Zara picks up the lipstick she put in with a

sadistic grin and waves it at Ben. "Fancy another make-over?" And we all shriek with laughter so sharp that Ash winces and covers his ears.

My item is a pack of cards – the ones I'd carried in my back pocket, pulling them out at the bus stop, at the Club, in McDonald's, practising my shuffle until I was better than Dean. This deck was my constant companion. I'd spent hours playing Solitaire and Nines, gambling pennies over Whist with Dean, laughing and yelling over games of Cheat and Pig and Go Fish ... It had been a wrench to put it in the box.

Sorrow wraps its sticky arms around me when I realise how little I've played those games since.

The last item left is a Happy Meal toy. Millie was so obsessed with collecting them that she wouldn't let us eat anywhere other than McDonald's.

I turn the tacky plastic figure onto its feet.

"Next envelope," I say. "Your turn, Ben."

13

Envelope no. 2

The second envelope is flat and Ben pulls out a folded piece of card with FREAKSOME FIVE FACT FILE on the front.

"Is that what you lot called yourselves?" Ash asks with a laugh. "Seems right enough."

But it's one thing to call yourself a freak, another for someone else to do it and none of us laugh along with the joke.

The card's been folded in a concertina and when Ben opens it out, a chain of paper dolls opens with it, one for each of us. It was an exercise we did with the younger kids at the Club – we'd made a giant chain of paper people reaching round the hall, each one a self-portrait. For this chain, instead of drawing our own 'doll', the other four of us worked on one doll while the victim watched and objected to every gleeful, mean observation we made about their clothes / hair / face.

Zara's doll has limbs in four different browns and we let Millie loose on her face, so her eyes are Manga-massive with long lashes and a mouth puckered into a shocked little 'o'. All the hairstyles are cut out and glued onto the dolls' heads like paper wigs, and someone got creative with Zara's, which has been cut from a model in a glossy magazine.

Zara's doll is holding hands with Millie's, and because Zara was in charge of Millie's, her doll's face actually looks a bit like her, down to the freckles across her cheeks. (There's also a red blob labelled 'Schubert' and I suspect Millie added that in.)

Dean's next, and his most distinctive feature is the note I wrote on his front that says – *Not to be confused with James Dean.*

We went to town on Ben – he was always the easiest to mock. His doll has a wonky nose and giant cut-out ears stuck on either side of his head. The clashing colours we used for his clothes aren't so different from the print of the shirt he's wearing tonight.

My doll is dull by comparison. I'm harder to caricature than Ben, although my skin has yellow-brown undertones and I'm wearing the stupid Spongeboob T-shirt I had on in my page of the photo album.

Under all the dolls is a mini fact file with key information, or what we thought was key when we were thirteen – favourite band, pet hates, what our Patronus would be. (We had to explain that one to Dean, who had zero interest in Harry Potter and wrote "Moggles don't need magic ghost animals", a misquote that distresses Zara as much now as it did when he wrote it. "It's *Muggles*, Dean!") I read my own fact file.

Favourite band – Depeche Mode

Pet hate – Anything Ben does/says, splinters that get under your nails, re-usable stickers (LIES!!!), door frames

Cartoon character you most identify with – Squidward

Best snack – Ready salted crisps dipped in salad cream

Thing you want be when you grow up – marine biologist

Patronus – Narwhal

It's funny how I'd forgotten about some of this – my obsession with being a marine biologist before I discovered how much I hated biology, whatever door frames had done to offend me – but I still love electro pop and eat crisps dipped in salad cream.

The others are marvelling over some of the things they'd written.

Ben's pretending to be embarrassed that he wanted to be a DJ and Zara's reassuring Ash that she no longer hates boys with diamond studs in their ears. But it's Dean I watch as he rests his finger lightly on the line where he wrote that he wanted to join the army.

It's hard to read what Millie wrote for that entry.

She wanted to be a nurse.

14

Envelope no. 3

Zara can see that Ash is getting antsy, so she nudges Dean to open the third envelope. Instead of emptying out the contents, he pulls out a sheet of paper.

"These are the rules," he says, and he looks round the group to see if any of us remember what they are.

Zara looks blank, Ben thoughtful and although I know it's something to do with dares, I can't remember what.

"Each one of us has dared another to do something," Dean says. "If you do the dare, then your challenger must tell you a secret – something that's happened since we made the box."

"Ooooh!" we chorus – even Ash.

"Alix is going first," Dean says. He grins at me as he pulls out the card with my name on. "Because I was the one who wrote hers."

Shit.

"So, Alix Yarinda Smith, your challenge, should you choose to accept it is ..." I start sweating during Dean's theatrical pause. "... Lick Ben's armpit."

"Oh my God!" I yell, covering my mouth in horror and speaking through my fingers. "That's gross."

"Yes, that *is* gross! I don't want my armpit violated by Alix's tongue." Ben's crossed his arms and tucked his hands in his armpits in hope of protecting them.

Dean shrugs. "Knew you wouldn't." And he

starts folding away the card as if he's going to move onto the next.

I'm not fooled. Dean was always playing this trick, knowing I'd do anything he asked if he made out I was too feeble to try.

And yet ...

"Hold up a minute," I say. "I said it was gross, not that I wouldn't do it."

Dean breaks out into a satisfied grin and murmurs, "That's my girl."

"I am not, and never will be your girl, Deano," I tell him. "Ben. Prepare the pit."

Ben protests a bit too much until Ash threatens to pin him down if he doesn't get on with it. Reluctantly, Ben pulls off his shirt and then, with a mutinous glare, removes his T-shirt. I feel a pang of sympathy for him, having to get half-naked sitting between Dean, who borders on scrawny, and

Ash, whose beefed-up biceps and chest boast of a hardcore gym habit.

"Sorry," I say, as I stand up to face him.

"I'm sorry too," Ben replies. "Thirteen-year-old Dean probably hadn't banked on me working up a sweat sprinting across the school yard."

It is exactly as revolting as everyone expected. After I've disinfected my mouth with neat vodka, I pour in the Coke and hand the bottle to Ben, who is fully clothed again and faintly disgusted.

"Tell us your secret." I point at Dean. "And make it good, or Ben and I will hurt you."

Dean is still wiping away tears of laughter as he settles down. There's a thoughtful pause and then, a moment later, his smile shifts to a scowl.

"I didn't do it."

"Do what?" Ben asks, confused, although it's me and Zara that Dean's watching when he replies.

"I know you all think I tried to trash the school," Dean says, and Ben's confusion fades – rumours don't have to take the fast train to London to travel. "But it was my brother Liam. I'd told him about the new computers in the library. He thought he could nick them and sell them on."

Dean looks around at the three of us, ignoring Ash entirely.

"Him and his mates tried to kick in the fire exit. That's why the alarms went off." He shrugs. "Liam was pissed about it and chucked a brick at a window. He was wearing my hoodie."

We wait for more, but Dean was never one for saying much. He leaves us to piece together the shards of information.

"Didn't you tell them?" Zara says, although whether 'them' means the school, the police or Dean's parents isn't clear.

Dean lets out a bitter bark of laughter. "That it was Liam? My brother who was old enough to be charged with vandalism? Who was already in trouble for selling stolen goods?" His voice is low as he picks at a piece of dried chewing gum on the floor of the roundabout. "I don't think my dad would have wanted me doing that."

"But he was fine with his youngest son getting chucked out of school for something he didn't do?" I'm filled with rage at the thought, but Dean doesn't seem bothered.

"Yeah. He was." Then he looks up at me. "And that's not why I got chucked out."

As Zara said, I wasn't there.

"Why then?" It's Ben who asks, Ben who had a good reason to leave his friends behind.

"I stopped going to class, caused trouble when I did," Dean says. "Couldn't see the point in giving a shit if no one else did." He shrugs and takes a short sharp breath before pulling out another card. "My turn."

It's Ben who thought of Dean's challenge. There's a sweet taped to the card that Dean has no problem eating.

"Thirteen-year-old me was stupid," Ben mutters as Dean sticks out his tongue to show it's all gone.

Ben screws up his face and reaches for a secret.

"I hate London," he says at last. It doesn't seem that big a deal, until I think of how much he goes on about it, online and in real life. "I hate it because it isn't *here*. When we moved, Mum told me I'd love it. She promised me we'd be living in a cool new flat, that I'd make new friends. But I liked my old house. My old friends." Ben pauses, eyes fixed on the dark of the fields beyond the park. "And then I moved and you forgot me."

I want to be affronted, but how can I be, when that's exactly what I did? Ben left and it was one less person for me to have to worry about. Neither Dean nor Zara have anything to say to this either. Ash looks like he wishes he'd already left to meet his mates at Bullion.

Ben looks back. "I'd rather blame a city for that than you."

"Ben ..." Zara reaches out and squeezes his hand, and when Ash opens his mouth to say something, Dean glares him into silence. "We didn't forget you," Zara says. "We lost touch because we were kids. And not just with you." Her eyes flicker to me and then to Dean.

"What about Millie?" I ask, thinking of all the emails she sent me.

Ben nods, miserable. "Yeah, she tried to stay in touch."

Instead of saying any more, Ben takes a long drink from the bottle and reaches for the envelope. "So what's my dare?"

Zara wrote Ben's and it's tame but timely, letting out the tension with laughter as Ben tries to put his toe in his ear. He's determined to get a secret out of Zara despite the limitations of his own body, and content to play the clown to make us feel better. I want to hug him and tell him I'm sorry, that I get it now – that I get *him*, but instead I suggest that he tries putting his right toe in his left ear.

Ben wins the dare, but the lift it gave the mood is lost when we see that Zara's crying.

"I never got to see Millie," she says. "Not until after she died." Her voice is as steady as the tears running down her cheeks. "I was supposed to go round, but I cancelled ..." It seems as if she's closing her eyes, the way she ducks her head, but I'm sitting close enough that I can see she's actually looking back, at the boy behind her. "I thought there'd be another time, but she was in hospital the next time I went to see her and she was too sick to see me."

Ash is resting one hand on her shoulder, but he's staring at the floor of the roundabout as if he's somewhere else. When Zara leans over to accept the last of my napkins, his hand slips from her shoulder.

He doesn't bother putting it back.

"Let's do my dare," Zara says after she's blown her nose.

Dean opens the card and raises his eyebrows. "Er ... you've got to kiss someone."

Zara's a bit taken aback, but before she has a chance to say anything, Ash speaks up. "Good job I'm here. You can kiss me."

Ben and Dean and I give Ash three identical dark looks, but it's Zara who speaks.

"I don't think that's what Millie had in mind when she wrote the dare," she says. "This isn't about you, Ash."

Ash's face clouds over. "If you think I'm going to sit here while you stick your tongue down another's guy's throat ..."

"For God's sake!" Zara turns to me and presses her lips to mine so fast there's no time for anyone to object. Not even me ... But this is nothing. No more than a fleeting touch that's as sexual as when my aunt and I misjudged our farewell air kiss at Christmas.

Which is a relief.

Zara sits back with her chin held high, ignoring Ash's flummoxed resentment. "I guess Millie can't tell us her secret or do her dare. Let's move onto the next envelope."

The others move around, passing the vodka

and sorting out all the rubbish we've made. Zara carries empty envelopes to the bin and Ben puts the things we're keeping back in the box. Ash gets up as though he's going to do something useful and then just stands there, stretching in a way that's designed to attract attention and saying how late it is.

Dean and I are the only ones who haven't moved and he stares across the roundabout at me. He knows I'm the person who wrote Millie's lost dare. That I've escaped having to tell them my secret.

A secret I'm certain he knows.

15

Envelope no. 4

The fourth envelope isn't as exciting as the others.

It's just a bunch of stuff we kept for no apparent reason. There's a game of Consequences Ben and Zara played at Club, that's half fart / burp / poo / sex puns and half a fairy tale in which a princess saves a prince but decides to marry the dragon. There's someone's wristband from the Seaside Sickness festival, the postcard I sent when I went away for a week to Magaluf. Items whose meaning has faded with time.

Ash's phone beeps and he sighs as he reads the message.

"The others are wondering where we are. Webby says that if we don't get there soon we won't get in." Ash gives Zara a meaningful look. "You said this wouldn't take long."

Zara isn't happy at him saying this, but she lays her hand on his arm, a butterfly settling on a bull. "I didn't know it would be so much fun seeing everyone. The next one's the letters we wrote to ourselves. I can take mine with me."

When she looks at us, she won't meet our eyes.

Envelope number five is the one I've been dreading and yet I'm the one expected to open it. Again. This one isn't padded, but made from thick cream paper and the writing on the front is neater. It's clear we took this envelope more seriously than the others, exactly as we're doing now. Everyone watches as I tuck a finger under the flap and tear.

Inside is another envelope.

"That's weird," I say. I was expecting five small envelopes, not another big one, and it's hard to pull it out because it's the same size as the one I've just opened. When I do, I see there's writing on the front.

"Oh ..." The word comes out on my breath, as if the sadness swelling within me has pushed it out.

"Alix?"

I force my gaze up to Ben, the one who's spoken, and then at the others.

"It's from Millie," I say, but I'm struggling to keep control of my voice and simply hand the envelope to Ben.

"'Hey guys,'" he reads, then swallows and closes his eyes for a beat. "'Hey guys, it's me, Millie. How's it going? Did you all do your dares? I wish I was there to see it. Who did Zara kiss? Bet it was Ben.'" Ben looks up at Zara, but she's crying too much to be embarrassed. "'Anyway. Are you wondering what to do with my letter? You should be. Do you give it to my parents? (NO!!!) But it would be a shame if *no one* read it, don't you think? I've already missed out on all the other things. (Except the photo album, I sneaked a peek at that one. We all look so *young*. I can't believe we thought Dean could pass for sixteen!) So I thought *you* could read my letter. On one condition – you all have to read your own out too. Out loud. All of you.'" Ben shakes his head. "She's underlined the word 'all' and drawn a picture of a stick figure doing an evil laugh," he says. He looks back and, in spite of everything, he laughs. "'P.S. Tell Alix that I emailed the school and they arranged for the caretaker to go up and get the box from where we'd hidden it. I bribed my sister and her boyfriend to sneak in and put it back. I bet she's the only one of you wondering about that instead of the letters.'"

Despite the tears streaming down my face, I laugh. She's right. I *was* wondering about that.

16
The letters

Zara's the first to speak. "I don't want to read my letter out."

I back her up, relieved. "Neither do I."

"Why not?" Ben asks, looking from me to Zara. "We wrote these when we were thirteen. No one's going to judge you for what's in there."

Zara gives Ash a nervous look that he interprets differently from me – he thinks she's asking for help. He swells into action, getting up to stand over us. "If Zara doesn't want to read it, she doesn't have to." He's already turned to walk towards his car, shouting back for Ben to give Zara her letter so they can go.

But when Zara turns to Ben, the envelope has gone.

"Where is it, Ben?" she asks and he pats the bulge beneath his shirt where he's tucked it into his belt.

"At least let's talk about it," Ben says, arms wide like the salesman he's going to turn into, looking to Dean for support.

"For fuck's sake," I mutter, and I get up and walk off towards the slide. "Do whatever you want."

I take the vodka bottle with me, ignoring Ben calling my name as Zara shouts at him to stop messing about. When I reach the slide, my legs fold under me until I'm sitting at the bottom of it, staring out at the sky as it deepens into the darker smudge of the sea.

A moment later, I hear footsteps behind me.

"Shift up." Dean kicks me gently and I move over. The slide is wide enough for three skinny kids to ride down holding hands. Less easy for three teenagers – me, Zara and Millie got stuck when we tried.

I drink from the bottle and hand it to Dean. I don't look at him, or speak. We pass the bottle back and forth a couple of times before Dean says, "It's been a weird night."

He's picking at the plaster on his arm and I turn to watch. The wound is bloody, but clean. "Grim," I say.

"I've had worse," he says, and he presses the plaster back over it. "Ben sent me over here to talk you into reading your letter."

"Why?"

"Because he thinks I've got more chance of convincing you than he has."

There's truth in that. Dean shouldn't have been the one I missed the most, but he was.

I'll miss him all over again once tonight's over.

"Why do you think Ben cares so much?" I ask.

Dean shrugs. "He likes to know what other people are doing."

I think of how hard it must have been for someone like Ben to feel cut out of our lives.

"And you?" I ask.

"I don't mind him knowing. I didn't have any secrets from you guys." It wasn't the question I asked and when Dean looks at me, his eyes are too bright for me to look right at them. "What is it you're so worried about sharing, Alix?" he asks.

"Nothing," I say too fast for him to believe me. "I just think it should stay private. All of it."

I know I could tell Dean that I'm gay and I know he wouldn't care.

But that's not what I'm worried about. Not any more.

"Why do you want us to do it?" I ask.

Dean takes the bottle back off me for a drink, swilling vodka round his mouth before he swallows. He has another slug, and another, until I take it from him.

"Because that's what Millie wanted," he says. "And I like making her happy. Sometimes it felt like she was the only person I could make smile."

I think about what I wrote in his birthday card and feel a jealous pang.

"What about me?" I sound so young when I say it.

Dean stares at me for a long moment. "You don't smile much, Alix. And when you do, it's not for me." There's something in the air between us, the weight of what he suspects and the truth I haven't told him. "Even when she was dying, when it must have been hard to be happy, she still smiled like she did when we were kids."

"You saw her?" I don't know why I'm surprised.

"Millie came round to tell me. Knocked on the door and asked for me. 'Hi, Mr Marshall, is Dean home? It's Millie Freberg. From Summer Club.' As if it hadn't been five years since either of us had been there." Dean grits his teeth. "When she saw me ..."

He puts his hand to his head, so his eyes are shaded for a moment. I hand him the bottle. When he tilts his head back to drink, his eyes glitter like the moon on the sea.

"No one sees me the way Millie did," he says. "I came here tonight because of her, not because of you or Ben or Zara. You promised her you'd get us here. I promised her we'd read the letters."

17

Fight

A shout from across the playground ruins our moment.

"ASHISH DUTTA, YOU ABSOLUTE ARSEHOLE!"

We're running over before I've even processed what's happening. There's Ben clutching his face while Ash shoves at him and Zara pulls on her boyfriend's polo shirt to no effect. Seconds later, Dean's on Ash's back with one arm around his neck, forcing him away from Ben. I'm shouting, trying to get between Ash and Ben, when Ash brings his arm back and cracks me in the side of the head with his elbow, knocking me to the floor.

My ear's on fire and the full force of the blow
rings in my head as I press my hand to the side of
my skull.

"Oh my God, you hit Alix!" Zara screams.

"I didn't –"

"Get away from her! Alix, are you OK?" Zara
crouches on the floor next to me, peering at where
my hand is, eyes wide with concern.

"I'm fine, ow, my ear ..."

I lift my hand away and Zara seems relieved to
see there's still an ear underneath – even if it is fire
engine red, judging by how hot it feels.

Ben reaches out the hand that's not clamped
to his nose and pulls me up. All four of us glare at
where Ash is standing. The fight has drained from
him, leaving only the arrogance. Next to me, I can
feel the tension rolling off Dean as he holds in his
temper the way he never could when he was younger.

"It was an accident." Ash glares at me like I'm to blame. "I don't hit girls."

"You shouldn't hit *anyone*," I say, standing shoulder-to-shoulder with Ben.

"All right, well, I'm leaving now, yeah?" Ash holds up his hands as if in surrender, as if that's enough of an apology for Ben's nose and my ear. He jerks his chin at Zara. "Come on, babe."

"No." The word fires out of her like a bullet. "You do *not* hit my friends and get to call me 'babe'!" Her face screws up in disgust, as if it would be a struggle to accept "babe" at the best of times. "Who the hell do you think you are?"

"I think I'm the chump who's driven you and your so-called friends around all night," Ash shoots back. "Who had to put up with you simpering over photos you'd forgotten existed, flirting with that jeb-end –" Ben edges a little further behind me as

Ash points at him. "– crying over a dead girl you've never once talked about –"

"Leave." Zara steps forward. "Now." When Ash doesn't move she pushes him towards the gate with sharp little shoves to his ribs, driving him back, step by step. "Go – *go away!* Get out of here! I don't want to see you any more. Never!"

She's backed Ash out of the park and now he's walking under his own steam, staring in surprise at how angry she is. How strong.

"Fine! I'm going, you fucking fruit loop." He hurries to open his car door, but before he gets in he shouts, "Good luck walking back to town!"

And then he slams the door, revs the engine, chucks the flash drive out the window and speeds off in a spray of gravel, nearly driving into the side of a passing van as he pulls out onto the road.

Zara watches him go, then she picks up the

flash drive and walks back towards us. "I did talk about Millie. *Loads*."

She pulls something out of the breast pocket of her jacket and hands it to Ben. "Tampons?" she says to a confused Ben. "For your nose."

Ben takes the tampons, still a bit baffled.

Dean wipes the rim of the bottle and passes it to Zara. "Drink? For your ... everything."

18

Ben's letter

We don't need to discuss the letters further, although the way Zara chugs at what's left of the vodka, I wonder what's in hers that she's so worried about reading.

I know what worries me. It's not letting these guys know I'm gay. I am not ashamed of that, and never have been, but I'm ashamed that I kept it from them. The memories in this box have brought us closer together and I'm scared that what I wrote in my letter will break us apart.

"So who's going first?" I ask. I don't want it to be me. Not this time.

"Ben," Zara says firmly.

Ben is a lot less certain now than he was before, but he opens his letter. I rest one hand on his shoulder so he can use the torch on my phone as a reading lamp.

Dear Ben of the Future

Here are the things I want to have done by the time you read this letter.

1. Kissed at least twenty girls
2. Passed my driving test FIRST TIME because neither of my parents did, the losers
3. Aced my exams (not too hopeful about that one, but if I don't write it down I might jinx things)
4. Scored a hat-trick in at least one match

Ben breaks away from his letter to shake his head. "I played in *goal*. What planet was I on when I wrote this?"

"What about the other stuff?" Zara asks, but Ben shakes his head slowly, so one bloodied tampon falls out of his nose. He pulls the other out and carries on.

5. Completed the hardest level of every *Battlefield* game ever made

6. Been to Ibiza

7. Touched a pair of fake boobs

8. Ridden Nemesis, preferably with the freaksome five

9. Punched someone who calls me "Fuckley" (just once, to see if it feels as good as I imagine)

10. Scored five-a-day

"That's a weirdly healthy goal, Benji," I say, but Dean's laughing hard and Ben is turning pink.

"He doesn't mean fruit and veg ..." Dean's almost crying now.

"I meant orgasms," Ben says in a sheepish voice. "I thought about wanking. A lot."

And we all laugh at him then, because who has *masturbation* goals?

Zara's the one who tells him to read out the rest.

11. **Grown a beard. Or at least a goatee. Or sideburns. But not a moustache. Girls don't like that**

12. **Had my nipple pierced (girls do like that)**

"No, Ben. They do not." (That's Zara.)

13. Learned how to use my decks

14. OK. And here's one I'll definitely have done before you read this letter, because I'm going to do it tomorrow. I've decided. I'm going to ask Millie out. To the cinema. Just us. I can't stop thinking about her.

Wish me luck.

Ben looks up from the end of his letter, stricken. It was the day after we put the box in the shaft that Ben's mum told him they were moving.

"I never asked her," he says.

19

Zara's letter

Zara and I put our arms around Ben and sandwich him in a hug. Dean reaches over to give him a consoling pat on the knee. I think back to Ben saying that Millie had tried to stay in touch with him and what that must have meant to a boy who wanted more than her friendship. Life is a list of missed opportunities – it seems cruel to remind Ben of this one.

When we pull apart, Zara reaches over for her letter and opens it up without discussion.

Dear me

I can't imagine being eighteen! How tall am I?
How skinny? Do I have a boyfriend? Have we done
it? Is he handsome? I've not even kissed anyone yet.
I don't think any of us have ... except maybe Dean,
who seems to have done everything.

"Had you?" she asks him, but Dean claims he
can't remember.

Alix might have done. I'm not sure. She's been
weird since she came back from Magaluf. When I
asked her if there were any fit boys in her hotel she
clammed up. I know Alix can be a bit secretive, but
I'll be really cross if she's kissed someone and not
told me. I'd tell her even if it was someone really
horrid like Snotto Wilson or a boy who was in the
year below or something ... But I guess just because

you tell someone all your secrets it doesn't mean they'll tell you theirs.

Zara pauses, then skims the next paragraph, before she looks up at me with eyes wide and wet with tears.

I don't know whether Alix would tell Millie ... Sometimes when it's the three of us I wonder if they wish I wasn't there, like maybe I'm in the way. It would be neater, wouldn't it, if there was four of us? Two boys and two girls.

She stops then, bowing her head and shaking as she sobs. Dean puts his arm round her and Ben squeezes her hand as I reach over, my own tears falling onto the roundabout. It's a while before Zara can read on.

Just read that bit back. It sounds a bit sad, doesn't it? I'm sure I'm just being paranoid. Papa is always telling me I worry too much. Does he still say that? Or do parents stop interfering once you turn eighteen? Probably not. Sonaya's been at university for a whole year and they still speak to her all the time on the phone and send her off with loads of food at the start of every term. She's getting a bit fat.

I should be about to go off to uni now, right? (My family seem to think I'll do Law but ... I don't know. I prefer stories to facts. English would be nice.) That must be weird. Leaving. I'm glad I'm not going anywhere now. I've had the best summer ever with Alix and Millie and Ben and Dean. When we go back to school I'm going to have someone to sit with in every single lesson. Even Music! I won't have to sit with Jessie or Cat or Sarah any more and pretend to know what they're talking about when Sarah says what she's done with her boyfriend, or lie when they ask me about how often I wax.

I don't need to pretend when I'm with my real friends.

I hope we all stay together until we open the box.

By the time Zara reads the last words, there isn't a person on the roundabout who isn't crying.

20

Alix's letter

"Me next," I say at last. I feel sick.

Zara nearly broke my heart with her letter and I owe her an explanation for how I behaved – and why I left – even if it will break her heart too. It is all here, all my thirteen-year-old fears, handwritten in a purple pen on a single side of A4. I keep my eyes down and read.

Dear future Alix

This is stupid. I've already binned three false starts because they sounded more like when school

makes you write letters to famous people you don't
know.

Although I don't know you, do I? It's not like I
can ask you questions and use your answers to fill
in the blanks. We're not in a *Star Trek* reboot (or if
we are, it's a crap one with no spaceships).

Still. If I could ask you anything, I'd ask you
this – do you have cool hair? I do not. It's long and
boring and I want to cut it all off, but I'm worried
what Mum will say. She thinks long hair looks
pretty, but I like girls with pixie crops and short
bobs with sharp bangs. I want to be one of them.

Sort of.

You know what that means, don't you? That I
don't just think it's their hair that's pretty. That it's
their everything.

That I think about kissing them.

But I have thought about kissing Dean. He's

got cool hair. (Maybe I'm a hair-sexual? Is that a thing? You can google it … if you still have Google in the future. A lot can happen in five years.) But that was an experiment. Kissing doesn't creep into my head when I see Dean the way it did every time I saw the Spanish girl with the sexy lips at our hotel in Magaluf. Or when I walk past Amber North in Year 11. Or Amber North's older, hotter sister. (And she has long hair.)

Actually, it's not just the kissing I think about. It's the 'and stuff'.

But not with Dean. That icks me out so much I can't even go there.

So why do I find it easier to *imagine* kissing a boy than telling my friends the truth?

Zara talks about boys all the time, about who she fancies, who might fancy her, or Millie, or (worse) me. They never think Amber North's hot sister might be an option. Girls aren't something they consider. But then, it's not like I ever talk about women's legs the way Zara talks about men's arms.

What if I tell them the truth and it changes things?

What if they start to have sleepovers without me the way the three of us have sleepovers without Ben and Dean? What if I'm wrong about all of this and it is just a phase and I ruin everything and they never want to speak to me ever again?

What if I find out that the people I love best in the world aren't what I thought they were? I mean, I'm not. Right?

I love them too much to test them. I love them too much to lie.

So you tell me – do I tell them?

I continue to stare at the paper.

"The end," I say, in case it isn't clear.

Ben's arm is a warm, comforting weight around my shoulders, but when Dean says my name I can't bring myself to look at him.

"It's OK," he says.

"It isn't ..." The tears that dried up while I focused on reading my letter well up once more. "I wish I'd told you."

It's not until Zara shuffles across, takes the letter from my hands and pulls me into a fierce hug that I let go completely.

"We understand, Alix," she says. Her hand is cool as she strokes the short hair on the nape of my neck.

"I'm sorry," I say into the shoulder of her jacket.

"You've nothing to apologise for." She squeezes me harder. "*Nothing*."

In Zara's arms, surrounded by my friends, I can finally release five years of guilt, five years of never knowing the truth. I'm overwhelmed with regret that I didn't trust them – overwhelmed with relief that I can now. I finally know that Zara and Dean and Ben have always been the people I hoped they were.

21

Dean's letter

I'm regretting giving away my lesbian napkins, but after I've wiped away the worst of my snot and tears on the bottom of my vest, I look over at Dean. He's been holding his letter right from the start, waiting for his turn.

He rips through the paper and reads it out.

The others are all taking this letter thing pretty seriously. Even Alix. Let's have a bet on what they're writing ...

Ben's easy. He'll be going on about his boner for

Millie that he thinks no one knows about.

Millie will be saying something nice about everyone and forget to put in anything about herself.

Zara's probably listing baby names in case she's married by now. She won't be. If anyone's going on to better things, it's Zara.

And Alix. God knows. Probably giving her future self some life advice. I've never met anyone quite so sorted as that one.

So that's them lot done.

Me? I just hope I'm not my dad. Or my brother.

"Shit." Dean tears the letter in half. His jaw is set, his eyes on fire.

"Dean?" I say, but he won't look at me – at any of us.

"*Shit.*"

"You're neither of them," I say. "You're you. Dean Marshall, the person I wanted to be when I grew up."

"And what did *I* grow up to be?" Dean glares at us. "I'm not a soldier in the army. I'm not going on to study anything. I'm still here, still hopeless – I'm everything he told me I'd become."

"You're our friend." Zara slips her hand into his. "We think you're worth something."

"In fact, I think you're brilliant," I say, and I nod at the box. "It's right there, in writing."

Dean looks at the box and then at me.

Ben taps his own letter as he thinks, then he says, "None of us have finished becoming who we want to be. I have a whole list to get through."

"Still thinking about wanking, Benji?" I say with a laugh.

"*Almost* a whole list to get through," he says.

He blushes, then turns to Dean. "Do you still want to join the army?"

The noise Dean makes isn't a 'yes', but it's not a 'no', either.

"Come round mine tomorrow," Ben says. "We can google what you need to do to get in. You've already got the haircut."

Dean narrows his eyes. "I'll think about it."

I look at the others – a silent pact to make sure he does more than think.

"Let's open Millie's letter," I say.

22

Millie's letter

Hey dorks.

In case you haven't already guessed, this isn't the letter I wrote when I was thirteen. (Seriously, you should be glad about that. It was SO DULL. I kept going on about my parents getting in my face about school work and then listed all my favourite things about you all. Which was sweet, but can be summarised as

Alix = brave

Ben = funny

Dean = sensitive (don't scoff, it's true and you know it)

Zara = kind

I wasn't trying to prank you or anything. But the thing about knowing you're about to die is that you spend a lot of time thinking about being alive. Way more than you do if you're actually going to live – *living* takes up so much brain space that it squishes out all the other stuff. The important things. Like when you felt like the best version of yourself. Who was there when you did. Whether you've been chasing that version of yourself ever since and never found her.

Because I needed you guys to show me.

I know why we all fell apart, that's just what happens. But things that fall apart can be put back together, right? Even if there's a piece missing.

I guess that's what tonight was about – just because I can't be there (because I'm dead, stupid stomach cancer), doesn't mean that I can't be the one to remind you that was the best summer of our lives. I've never felt happier than when you lot were the most important people in my life.

Have you?

OK, so I'm crying now, I really *really* wish I could be there to see you all. I want to do my dare. I want to see if Alix can still shuffle cards. If Zara has worn something completely impractical for climbing onto a school roof. If Ben is as cute in real life as he is in all the pictures he posts online. If Dean is capable of smiling instead of scowling when you all take a selfie.

Fuck. I really fucking hate fucking stomach fucking cancer.

I love you guys.

Always have. Always will.

23

Night over

Dean picks up the empty vodka bottle and hurls it across the playground with a roar. No one says anything, but I hold out my arms and he steps in for a hug. He squeezes me tight as I cry into his shoulder. Behind me, Ben rests a hand on my back and hands me one of the tissues that fell out when I opened her letter.

His face is blotchy and wet as he says, "Trust Millie to know this would happen."

When Dean hugs Ben, he holds him so tight that I can see where his fingers are digging into Ben's back. And then I'm holding Zara. I no longer think she feels small and fragile as I draw from her the strength I need.

It's Zara who gets it together first.

"So," she says, her voice hoarse. "I think Millie would be pretty annoyed if we just spent the night crying in a kids' play park."

I look at the other two. "I don't want to go home yet," I say. What I mean is that I'm not ready to leave these guys. Not yet. Not ever.

"Me neither," Zara says. "So let's go out and celebrate."

Ben laughs. "Millie would like that."

"Yeah." Dean nods. "She would."

We all look at each other, then down at the faraway town. It's a long walk now the buses have stopped ... but then my phone bloops a message into the silence. It's Faith.

Hey you, is everything OK? Want me to come and pick you up?

I smile down at my phone and then up at my friends.

"Do we want my girlfriend to come and give us a lift?"

Ben and Zara nod fervently, but it's Dean I'm looking at, and the way he's smiling at me makes me smile right back.

I'm glad I kept my promise.

Acknowledgements

With thanks to everyone at Barrington Stoke – Mairi, Emma, Jane, Kirstin, Julie-ann (and anyone who's worked behind the scenes without me knowing!) – my agent Jane Finigan, everyone on Twitter who volunteered information on how to stash cigarettes and tampons, and one extra special thank you to Charlie Morris for her advice.

Are you a book eater or a book avoider – or something in between?

This book is designed to help more people love reading. It's a moving, uplifting, emotional story by a fantastic author, with a gorgeous cover, shiny foil and more for book lovers to treasure. At the same time, it has clever design features to support more readers.

You may notice the book is printed on heavy paper in two colours – black for the text and a pale yellow Pantone® for the page background. This reduces the contrast between text and paper and hides the 'ghost' of the words printed on the other side of the page. For readers who perceive blur or movement as they read, this may help keep the text still and clear. The book also uses a unique typeface that is dyslexia-friendly.

If you're a book lover, and you want to help spread the love, try recommending *Unboxed* to someone you know who doesn't like books. You never know – maybe a super-readable book is all they need to spark a lifelong love of reading.

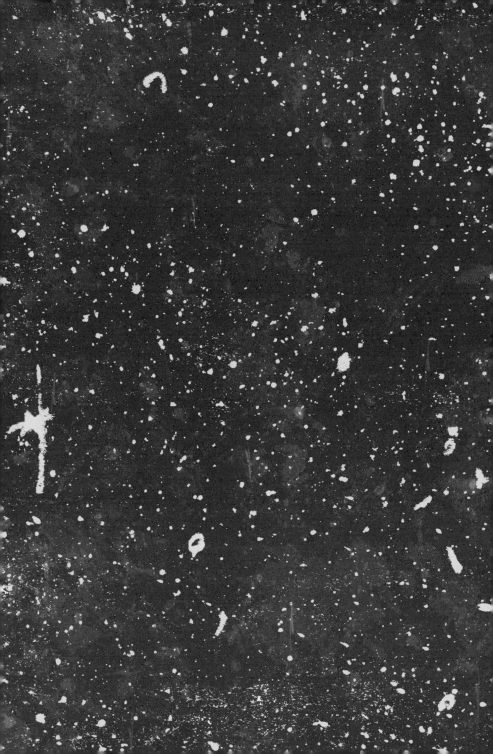

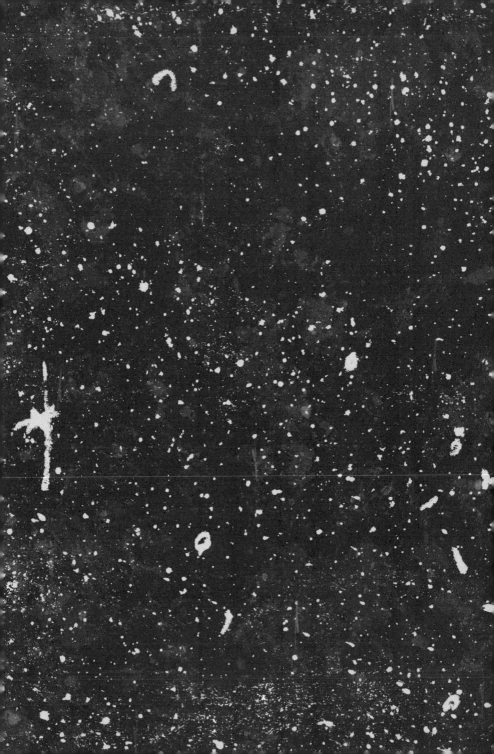